WRITTEN BY **Susan Hughes**   ILLUSTRATED BY **Suharu Ogawa**

Hooray for Trucks!

OWLKIDS BOOKS

"It's your big day, trucks. Time to shine!
One by one, all of you, GET IN LINE!"

"Come on, now. You need to wash.
Let's get going—slather and slosh.

"You there, Loader. And Bulldozer, too.
Come get clean—yes, ALL of you!

"Yes, you, Backhoe.
You too, Plow.

"We're heading off soon,
so get rolling now!"

"Excavator! Roller!
Flatbed Truck!
What's going on?
Your wheels CAN'T be stuck!

"Let's GO, trucks—hurry!
Over here!
All of you—that's it.
GET IN GEAR!"

But the trucks don't move. The trucks don't budge.
Trucks **LIKE** dirt and mud and sludge!

Trucks like one thing: trucks like **work**.
Flatten that soil and haul that dirt.

Bucket Truck, Pickup Truck, old and new—
trucks want to move. Trucks want to **DO!**

Carry those bricks. Lift that beam.
Trucks work alone or as a team.

To be soaked and lathered,
scrubbed high and low?
That's just boring—
so **no, no, NO!**

"Getting clean might seem a bore.
But no, it's an IMPORTANT chore!

"Wash away that dirt.
Drive away that rust.
To keep you rolling,
it's A MUST!"

Wait–what? Getting clean is **ALSO** work?

Then the trucks will help. Trucks **NEVER** shirk!

Bobcat, Cement Mixer,
rub-a-dub-dub!

Forklift, Grader,
sponge and **scrub!**

Splash and spray,
slather and slosh,
dunk and swish—
wash, wash, WASH!

Sparkling, gleaming,
rubbed and **buffed,**

the trucks are pleased—
the trucks are **chuffed!**

"Now, come on, trucks. TIME TO GO!

Will you form a tidy row?"

The trucks are quiet.
The trucks are still.
Then ...

And guess who's ready to help them shine?

Kids, kids, kids—carrying banners and signs!

People in the sunshine, people in the shade.
People line the streets sipping pink lemonade.

There! Do you hear that noisy serenade?
Get ready, get set for the ...

Owlkids Books acknowledges the financial support of the Canada Council for the Arts, the Ontario Arts Council, the Government of Canada through the Canada Book Fund (CBF) and the Government of Ontario through the Ontario Creates Book Initiative for our publishing activities.

Published in Canada by
Owlkids Books Inc.
1 Eglinton Avenue East
Toronto, ON M4P 3A1

Published in the United States by
Owlkids Books Inc.
1700 Fourth Street
Berkeley, CA 94710

Library and Archives Canada Cataloguing in Publication

Title: Hooray for trucks! / by Susan Hughes ; illustrated by Suharu Ogawa.
Names: Hughes, Susan, 1960- author. | Ogawa, Suharu, 1979- illustrator.
Identifiers: Canadiana 20210389664 | ISBN 9781771474672 (hardcover)
Classification: LCC PS8565.U42 H66 2022 | DDC jC813/.54—dc23

Library of Congress Control Number: 2021951815

Edited by Jennifer Stokes
Designed by Diane Robertson

Manufactured in Shenzhen, Guangdong, China, in March 2022, by WKT Co. Ltd.
Job #21CB3198

A   B   C   D   E   F

For Jasper Howse—hooray for trucks! —S.H.

To my parents, Misuzu and Kazuho, the best parade conductors —S.O.

Publisher of Chirp, Chickadee and OWL
www.owlkidsbooks.com

Owlkids Books is a division of bayard canada